To Caroline, my little sis'
and my favorite saltimbanco!
V. M.

To Serge
V. H.

With special thanks to Christine Pinault of the Picasso
Administration for her help in the elaboration of this project.

© for the original French edition: L'Élan vert, Paris, 2012
© for the English edition: 2013, 2nd printing 2016, Prestel Verlag, Munich · London · New York
A member of Verlagsgruppe Random House GmbH
Neumarkter Strasse 28 · 81673 Munich
© for the work by Pablo Picasso: Fondation Picasso, 2012.
Photo: © 2016. Digital image, The Museum of Modern Art, New York/Scala, Florence
© Fondation Picasso, 2016

Prestel Publishing Ltd.
14-17 Wells Street
London W1T 3PD

Prestel Publishing
900 Broadway, Suite 603
New York, NY 10003

Library of Congress Control Number: 2016937476

English translation: Agathe Joly

Copyediting: Cynthia Hall
Typesetting: Meike Sellier
Production management: Astrid Wedemeyer
Printing and binding: TBB, a.s.

Verlagsgruppe Random House FSC® N001967
The FSC-certified paper *Condat Matt Périgord*
was supplied by Papier Union.

Printed in Slovakia

ISBN 978-3-7913-7151-1
www.prestel.com

The Three Musicians

A Children's Book
Inspired by Pablo Picasso

Véronique Massenot
Vanessa Hié

Prestel
Munich · London · New York

The beast was terrifying.
A wolf! some said.
But **a monstrous wolf,** bigger
and stronger than a fighting bull.

In the kingdom of Mirador few had seen the beast
in the flesh. Few had faced it…
But all, young and old, knew its name.
A name full of menace. And all, from the least courageous to the bravest,
trembled when they heard **"Fire-Mouth!"**

This name was all that **King Minus of Mirador** would talk about.
Fire-Mouth here, Fire-Mouth there…
—Fire-Mouth had swallowed another calf, devoured two lambs,
flayed three horses… without a single bone left behind.
—Do you understand, by Jove?
We must hunt Fire-Mouth down!

King Minus could only think
of one thing: the beast.
Nothing else could hold his interest.
Neither knowledge, nor nature…
Not even love. *Nada!*

For him, all that mattered was Fire-Mouth.
—If you let the beast do what it pleases,
one day it will come and devour your
children right out of your arms.

Yikes...
Those speeches were scary!

Yet, instead of watching out day and night,
instead of keeping a weapon at hand, of always marching in step,
many subjects of the kingdom would have liked, once in a while,
to think of something else.
And so, as it turned out, one bright April morning,

four strange silhouettes

appeared in the city.
They slipped into the streets, filled with joy,
drawing the mark of their four mysterious profiles
on the sad and bare walls.

When the king's bells chimed
at ten o'clock,
one of the odd characters
gallantly addressed the crowd
in the middle of the town square.

—Hear, hear, good people!
he cried out in a bold and almost
sing-song voice.
Many thanks for your hospitality!
Here are my companions,
Pierrot and Capucin.
My name is Harlequin,
and here is Cocoa-pod…
named for his chocolate coat!
We are saltimbancos: musicians,
comedians, jugglers, and a circus dog.
We come to entertain you.
What tune would you like to hear?

Passers-by had gathered.
Clearly suspicious, but intrigued.
Windows had opened
and eventually, every balcony was filled with onlookers.
But still, the crowd remained silent.

Come, what dance would you like to do?
Don't be shy! A slow sarabande or a wild farandole?
A crazy fandango or a distinguished tango? Or perhaps you
would rather have a seguidilla… or a flamenco from Seville?

At last, someone spoke up:
—Forgive us, **we never dance.**
Since the beast arrived… Fire-Mouth…
we live in fear and no longer have the heart to dance.

Tongues loosened and the people began to talk
about the calves, the lambs, the horses,
and one day, perhaps… the children!
Others spoke of rounds, spears,
halberds, and of this monster…
which would not show its face.

—My friends, answered Harlequin, you are trying
to face the beast, to hunt it, to kill it… in vain.
But… have you thought of taming it?
Let's try to charm it! Who knows? Perhaps,
Fire-Mouth will respond to music?
And so the acrobats got to work.
—This tune is a passacaglia! **Sing,
dance… have some fun!**
It was a great success. While the three musicians
were playing, Cocoa-pod pretended to be the beast,
frightening and ferocious. With all these arpeggios,
trills and tremolos… it slowly began to soften,
until finally it was wiggling on his back,
asking to be petted! People were laughing
until their sides ached. **What a show!**

From that day on, life in the kingdom of Mirador changed.
People learned to sing, to dance, and to speak openly of their fears,
their happiness, and all those things that make the heart beat faster.
They soon saw that outside, the spade had replaced the spear.
And they saw young sprouts shooting up from the rocks
and green oases adding color to the scenery. Then, in the coolness
of the gardens, came the time of courtship.
People gave each other flowers, recited poems…
and exchanged kisses. As for Fire-Mouth,
no one heard from him…

—Argh… This does not please me at all! stormed, grumbled,
and growled the king in his palace. What a bunch of idiots:
so they're not scared anymore?
They won't listen? They'd rather fool around
with those three characters and their nasty dog?!
Minus of Mirador thought he was a clever man:
—I have a great idea that will put everything back in order!
One night, his ferocious bodyguards captured Cocoa-pod,
knocked out a bull, and then smeared red paint
like blood on one's mouth and the other's throat.
—Hahaha! So you enjoy a good show? sniggered
the contemptuous king to himself. Well then,
let's see what you think of this one…

The sun had just risen when the alarm was raised. The bull
lay in the middle of town square. The news spread faster through the streets
than a flame on a long wick.

—Oh no! Fire–Mouth has struck again!

—Will we never know peace?

Then King Minus appeared. Raising his chin and looking superior,
he felt triumphant. Behind him, in a dreadful
iron cage, his guards dragged in the poor and terrified Cocoa-pod.
People trembled in fear.
—Can it be? The circus dog?
—Fire-Mouth finally unmasked?
—The beast certainly had us fooled!
—Where are its masters! They deceived us…
—Let's arrest them! Judge them! Punish them!
People felt betrayed and their anger was rising…

All of a sudden, in the midst of this furious brouhaha
rose a young girl's voice, clear and wise.
She was standing at the edge of a window and
holding up a metal pot dripping with red paint:
—I saw everything! Cocoa-pod isn't guilty,
It's a trick! Look this isn't blood, it's paint!

Confused, the people didn't know what to believe…
That is, until the bull woke up!
—It's alive! But… Then…
—So the king is the one who lied!

What happened next
still makes people laugh today...
The bull rose to its feet in a fury and
charged at Minus and his guards. No need to say
how quickly they snatched up their things and
fled from sight.

From that day on, this hilarious scene has been played each year in the town square on **the feast of Mirador**... which is no longer a kingdom.

"Minus, you have learned at your own expense, that putting on a show is an art that, alas, you cannot improvise," sing Harlequin, Pierrot, and Capucin while Cocoa-pod collects all the hurrahs and the bravos, perhaps even —who knows—those of a music-loving, charmed, and enchanted Fire-Mouth...

Three Musicians
Pablo Picasso

1921
Oil on canvas
200.7 x 222.9 cm
The Museum of Modern Art (MoMA),
New York

Pablo Picasso

Who are these three musicians?

Harlequin, Pierrot, and Capucin are three characters from la commedia dell'arte. Picasso paints them wearing masks, standing behind a table with their instruments. Pierrot blows a clarinet, Harlequin in the center plays the guitar, and Capucin holds the score. Underneath the table, a brown dog as dark as a shadow is lying down. We can only see its legs and its head.

Is this work a "papier collé"?

No. But this large work in oil on canvas actually does look like papier collé. Like the objects that surround them, the shapes and colors of the three musicians give the impression of bits of paper that have been glued together. Picasso chose this humoristic and poetic way of painting to celebrate theater and music. The characters look like puppets in a pantomime, with their colorful costumes and masks.

Why has Picasso painted them?

Picasso was very interested in musicians and the commedia dell'arte. He represented Harlequin's character many times, often using his son as a model (*Paul as Harlequin*, 1924). He also painted clowns and saltimbancos, musicians and their instruments, in *The Guitarist* in 1910, *Mandolin and Guitar* in 1924, and *Guitar* in 1924 as well. In 1921, he painted two versions of *The Three Musicians*, a subject that evidently inspired him.